I AM READING

THE PRINCESS and the PETS

ANGELA KANTER

Illustrated by
MADDY McCLELLAN

KINGFISHER

KINGFISHER
An imprint of Kingfisher Publications Plc
New Penderel House, 283-288 High Holborn
London WC1V 7HZ
www.kingfisherpub.com

First published by Kingfisher 2007
2 4 6 8 10 9 7 5 3 1

Text copyright © Angela Kanter 2007
Illustrations copyright © Maddy McClellan 2007

The moral right of the author and illustrator has been asserted.

A CIP catalogue record for this book
is available from the British Library.

ISBN: 978 0 7534 1467 5

Printed in China

1TR/0307/WKT/SCHOY(SCHOY)/115MA/C

Contents

"Why can't I have a pet?" Princess Mina asked the queen.

"Because they make a mess," said the queen.

"So does she," said Princess Mina, looking at her teenage sister, Princess Tina. She was slumped on the floor in the middle of a pile of magazines and half-empty mugs.

"Why can't I have a pet, Daddy?" asked Princess Mina.

"They smell," said the king.

"And they leave hairs everywhere."

"So does Princess Tina!" said Princess Mina. "She pongs!"

She turned up her nose at her sister, who was only just visible through a haze of perfume and hairspray. It was like an explosion in a flower shop.

"And look —" said Princess Mina,
pulling a handful of hairs from the royal
beanbag, where Princess Tina had been
sitting and brushing her long hair.

8

"I'll ask Nanny for a pet," thought
Princess Mina. "She's a softie."
She edged over to the rocking chair,
where Nanny was knitting a long scarf.

"You'd like a cat or a dog, wouldn't you,
Nanny?" cooed Princess Mina.

9

"Try this on, dear," said Nanny, wrapping the scarf around the Princess's neck ten times, until she could hardly breathe.

"It's for your birthday present," Nanny said cheerfully.

"But I really wanted a . . . oh, never mind," said Princess Mina. "It's lovely, Nanny."

Princess Mina felt like crying. "I'm never
going to get a pet," she said with a sigh.
Then she had a brilliant idea.

Chapter Two

"I'm going to ask my Fairy Godmother for a pet," thought Princess Mina. "That's what they're for, after all, granting wishes."

She went up to her room.

All her t-shirts were hanging out of her chest of drawers and her books were all over the bed.

Her crown was lying on the dressing
table. It was rather bent, as if it had
been tried on by someone whose head
was really too big.

Princess Mina marched downstairs
again, to see Princess Tina.

"You've been borrowing my stuff
without asking again, haven't you?"
said Princess Mina.

"Yeah . . ." said Princess Tina. She was
stuffing her face with marshmallows.
Princess Mina's marshmallows. The ones
that Nanny had given Princess Mina last
week, as a reward for helping to unravel
her knitting wool.

17

"And don't go telling Mum and Dad or
that stupid fairy godmother of yours that
I've used your stuff," said Princess Tina,
"or I'll pull your hair so hard you have
to get Nanny to knit you a wig!

"And you're never going to get a pet from
anyone for your birthday, ever, because
all pets make me sneeze! So there!"

And Princess Tina stomped out
of the room. Ever since her
boyfriend, Prince Bertram, had
been turned into a frog, she'd
been in a really bad mood.

Princess Mina tidied up the mess, and then she got out her mobile and texted her Fairy Godmother. After a few moments, her Fairy Godmother texted back.

"Too busy making toads to visit. What do you want? Will text you a spell."

Making toads? Did she mean making toast? Mina wondered. Her fairy godmother was not very good at texting and often pressed the wrong keys.

Princess Mina
texted back.
"Would like pet
for birthday."

At once, her Fairy Godmother
sent back a spell.
Princess Mina read it out carefully.

There was a loud bang
and the castle shook.

"Oh no," thought Princess Mina.
"Princess Tina's plugged her hair
straighteners into the washing-machine
socket again."

But it wasn't that. It was something
much more exciting.

Chapter Three

The pets were arriving!

In the kitchen, kittens jumped out of the blackberry pie that the king was making.

In the lounge, puppies popped up on the
sofa next to the queen, and chewed up
her slippers as she snoozed in front of
the news.

In the bedroom, two glistening goldfish swam around and around Nanny's false teeth.

And in the bathroom, Princess Tina reached for the soap and found herself holding a rather magnificent, shining turtle!

For a while, all that could be
heard in the palace was screaming
and shouting – with a few
miaows and yelps.

Princess Mina ran from room to room,
greeting all her lovely new pets.

But an hour later, she
didn't feel quite so happy.

"No birthday cake unless you get rid of the pets, I'm afraid," said the king, scraping his blackberry pie into the bin.

"This pie is full of cat hair.
I'll never be able to make
you a birthday cake with all
these kittens in the kitchen."

"The puppies will have to go, too," said the queen. "My slippers will never be the same."

Nanny tried to
say something . . .

. . . but spat out
a goldfish instead.

33

Princess Tina was the angriest of them all.
The turtle had made her come out in spots
and when she'd gone to steal some of
Princess Mina's make-up to cover them up,
she picked up a powder puff and found it
was a hamster.

And then she realized that perhaps it hadn't been such a good idea to eat those "chocolate drops" she'd found next to Princess Mina's bed.

"Get rid of all these pets," she hissed to her sister.

A boa constrictor hissed back peacefully from under the bed.

Princess Mina just did
not know what to do.

Chapter Four

"Get rid of all these pets!" said Princess
Tina, in a more wobbly voice this time.
"Or – or – I'll get my fairy godmother to
turn you into a frog."

But talking about frogs reminded Princess Tina of her dear Prince Bertram, who was doomed to live as a little green creature in the pond. She started to cry and completely forgot about being mean to Princess Mina any more.

Princess Mina
began to feel sorry
for her sister. She
texted her fairy godmother again.

"Please send spell
to take away the
pets," she typed.

Immediately, her fairy
godmother sent back
this message:

"A spell to take
away the pest."

Another typing mistake, Princess Mina supposed. She read out the spell carefully.

There was another huge bang and the castle shook again.

Was everything fixed now?

Chapter Five

The fairy dust settled. Princess Mina looked around. The king came into the room, with a handful of kittens.

"I suppose they're quite sweet really," he said. "They can stay."

The queen came running
in, with the puppies at her
heels.

"They're all right," she
said. "I'm training them
to bring me my
newspaper and slippers."

Nanny came in. She had found a nice bowl for the goldfish.

"I'm going to knit a lovely goldfish-bowl cosy to keep the water warm," she said.

It looked like the spell hadn't worked. Princess Mina waited for her big sister to say something horrible. But Princess Tina was nowhere to be seen.

Suddenly, Princess Mina realized what was wrong. "A spell to take away the *pest,*" she remembered. "It really did take away the pest. Princess Tina was a pest. But I wonder what's happened to her."

Out in the palace grounds, an amazed
Frog Prince (once known as Bertram)
was happily saying hello to his delighted
Frog Princess Tina . . .

About the Author and Illustrator

Angela Kanter sits in a newspaper office all day drinking coffee, and writes children's books at night, when it's really past her bedtime. She has no pets, but her two daughters dream of owning a cat or dog, or maybe a peacock . . .

Maddy McClellan lives in Brighton. She says, "As a child, I was always begging my parents for pets. At one point, I had a white pony, a dog, two rabbits, four guinea pigs, a hamster, and even a couple of goldfish!" At the moment her son Inigo keeps her busy, but she does have a very fat black cat called Minouche.

Tips for Beginner Readers

1. Think about the cover and the title of the book. What do you think it will be about? While you are reading, think about what might happen next and why.

2. As you read, ask yourself if what you're reading makes sense. If it doesn't, try rereading or look at the pictures for clues.

3. If there is a word that you do not know, look carefully at the letters, sounds, and word parts that you do know. Blend the sounds to read the word. Is this a word you know? Does it make sense in the sentence?

4. Think about the characters, where the story takes place, and the problems the characters in the story faced. What are the important ideas in the beginning, middle and end of the story?

5. Ask yourself questions like:
Did you like the story?
Why or why not?
How did the author make it fun to read?
How well did you understand it?

Maybe you can understand the story better if you read it again!